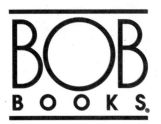

LEVEL 1

50-250 WORDS

# Buddy to the Rescue

by LYNN MASLEN KERTELL
illustrated by SUE HENDRA

SCHOLASTIC INC.

*Dedicated to the firefighters of Station 18,*
*Seattle, Washington*

ISBN 978-0-545-38273-1

10 9 8 7 6 5 4 3 2 1          12 13 14 15 16 17/0

Printed in the U.S.A.     40
First printing, November 2012

"Do you hear that? says Anna.

Jack and Anna run out the door.

They hear horns. They hear drums.
A fair has come to town.

"Let's get Buddy and go!" says Anna.

Anna and Jack and Mom and Dad
walk to the fair.

Mom gets tickets.
Jack goes on a ride.

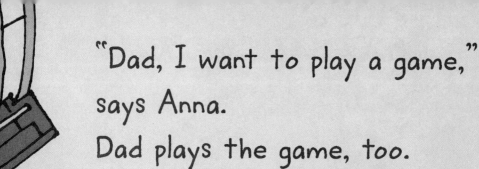

"Dad, I want to play a game,"
says Anna.
Dad plays the game, too.

"Ruff, ruff," says Buddy.

"Buddy, you cannot have a hot dog," says Anna.

11

Buddy looks big.
Buddy looks small.
Buddy looks like a funny dog.

"Let's go on the bumper cars," says Anna.

*Boom! Bang!*

Anna and Jack crack and crash
their cars.

"Ruff, ruff," says Buddy.

"Buddy, no! You cannot have a hot dog," says Anna.

# Buddy barks.

Buddy runs to the hot dog stand.

Anna sees smoke.
Anna sees fire.

"Dad! Dad!" shouts Anna.

Sound the alarm. Ring the bell.

Call 911.
There is a fire at the
hot dog stand!

The fire truck is on its way.
The siren is very loud.
Red lights flash.

# The fire truck pulls up.

Water sprays. Smoke puffs.

Buddy is safe. The fire is out.
The hot dog man is safe, too.

Buddy is a hero.
Buddy saw the fire first.

# Anna gives Buddy a hug.

The firemen pat Buddy.

"Buddy, now you can have
your hot dog," says Anna.